Je
the
Gnome

First published in the United Kingdom in 2018 by
The Choir Press

ISBN 978-1-911589-76-1

Jerome the Gnome

DENISE SMITH

The Choir Press

JANUARY

Hello, Jerome, are you going to play?
Tell me what's happening – what you'll do today.

◎◎

Jerome wakes one morning, his room is so bright.
He looks through his window and oh! What a sight!
The ground is all covered in white fluffy snow.
He gets up so quickly as outside he must go.

His gloves and his wellies, his coat and his hat.
He runs out to build a snowman so fat,
His eyes made of berries, his nose a big stick.
A hat and Dad's scarf should just do the trick.

Jerome made a wish that his snowman could play,
Make snowballs and throw them on this winter's day.
Then as the snow fell Jerome's wish came true.
The snowman bent down and a snowball he threw.

Jerome, so surprised, fell down in the snow,
Looked up at the snowman who started to glow.
'Hello,' said the snowman. 'Let's play in the snow,
For when the snow melts I just have to go.'

Jerome and the snowman they laughed and played,
They built a snow castle with a bucket and spade.
The friends they had fun, the snow it did fall,
Not aware they were watched from over the wall.

There stood a fairy; she watched from afar.
Her little wings glistened like a sparkling star.
Then all of a sudden there appeared in the snow
A bright shining light that started to glow.

Jerome and the snowman they watched in surprise
As the sparkling light shone bright in their eyes.
There in the snow stood an angel so bright.
Her wings were like feathers – what a magical sight.

The angel she came from a place far away
Where all special snowmen were taken to stay.
When the snow melts and the sun warms the ground
Not one single snowman can ever be found.

Jerome he looked on as the snowman did go
With the magical angel, into the snow.
Jerome he was sad to see his friend go.
'Don't cry,' said the fairy. 'I want you to know

'That I have been watching from over the wall.
I too had a snowman; he was jolly and tall.
The snow angel came and she took him away
To the place in the sky where all snowmen stay.

'Our snowmen, I'm sure, will meet up in that land.
The angel she took them – one in each hand.'
Jerome and the fairy they had so much fun
With the magical snowmen in the snow and the sun.

◎◎

Goodbye, Jerome, thanks for sharing your day,
For letting me know the things that you play.

FEBRUARY

Hello, Jerome, are you going to play?
Tell me what's happening – what you'll do today

◎◎

Jerome was outside one cold frosty day.
He decided the lake was a good place to play.
He checked with his mummy: 'Is it OK to go?'
'Yes, but take a map with you; the way it will show.

'Take care by the road and put on your big coat
And stay far away from the old Billy Goat.
Follow the map past the Billy Goats' home.
Don't go to places that you've not been shown.

'What is your plan when you get to the lake?'
'I really don't know; perhaps a camp I will make.
I'll build it with twigs and cover with moss.
Or maybe the bridge on the lake I will cross.'

'Well, just you be careful and make sure you're good,
And don't you come home all covered in mud.'
Before very long Jerome reached the lake.
He sat on the bridge to take a short break.

He gazed down below at the water to see
The water had frozen – what fun this could be.
The gnome sat and thought of what he could do
When there stood a fairy right out of the blue!

'I have an idea,' said Jerome's little friend.
'We could put some skates on and then could pretend
That we are about to see the Ice King.
We could take him a gift and a song we could sing.'

'Oh, that sounds like fun,' said the gnome with a smile,
'But I haven't worn skates for such a long while.
I think you may find I'll fall over, you see,
And you and the King would both laugh at me.'

'Come on,' said the fairy, 'I know you will stand,
For I'll sprinkle your skates with magical sand.'
The fairy she cast a magical spell
And the two little friends they skated so well.

All round the lake they danced and they sang.
Even the snowdrops their little bells rang.

As Jerome and the fairy danced to and fro
The Ice King he watched them and wanted to know
If the fairy would cast her magical spell
So he could have skates and dance just as well.

'Of course I'll do magic so you can join in.'
Jerome he watched on as the King did a spin.
He danced round the lake, forward and back,
When all of a sudden was a very loud crack!

The three of them stopped – what could it be?
And there on the lake they could all plainly see

The ice it had broken; a crack had appeared.
'Oh no!' said the fairy. 'This is just as I'd feared.

'Come quickly and hold on tight to my hand.'
With a few magic words and her magical sand
The three of them stood quite safe on the ground,
All of them happy, all safe and sound.

'I have had so much fun today on the lake.'
The Ice King was laughing and trying to take
His magical skates off his very big feet.
'I hope you two friends come again and we meet

'Just here on the bridge that goes over the lake,
And next time you come I will bring a big cake.
Now you two must leave, for you have far to go.
The weather is changing – it's looking like snow.

'Follow the map past the Billy Goats' home.
Farewell, little fairy and little Jerome.'
The two little friends they waved to the King,
Then followed the map past the slide and the swing,

Back to the garden where the little gnome played.
They wished that the King could maybe have stayed.

Jerome he knew well that the King must return
Back to his people so they could all learn
Where the iced lake was hidden from sight
So they could all go and skate in the night.

'Jerome,' said the fairy, 'will you be mine?
For today is the day of St Valentine,
When really good friends promise to be
For ever together – please let it be me.'

The little gnome blushed, so happy was he
Jerome and the fairy together would be,
For deep in his heart the gnome really knew
That he and the fairy would for ever be true.

The fairy she flew back home, on a dove,
Knowing Jerome was her only true love.
The little gnome watched as she flew through the sky
And blew her a kiss as she waved him goodbye.

The gnome walked back home singing a song.
He knew his best friend would not be gone long,
For before she had flown they promised to meet
The very next day at the park on the seat.

The tired little gnome got ready for bed.
He was back in his house, its roof white and red.

◎◎

Goodbye, Jerome, thanks for sharing your day,
For letting me know the things that you play.

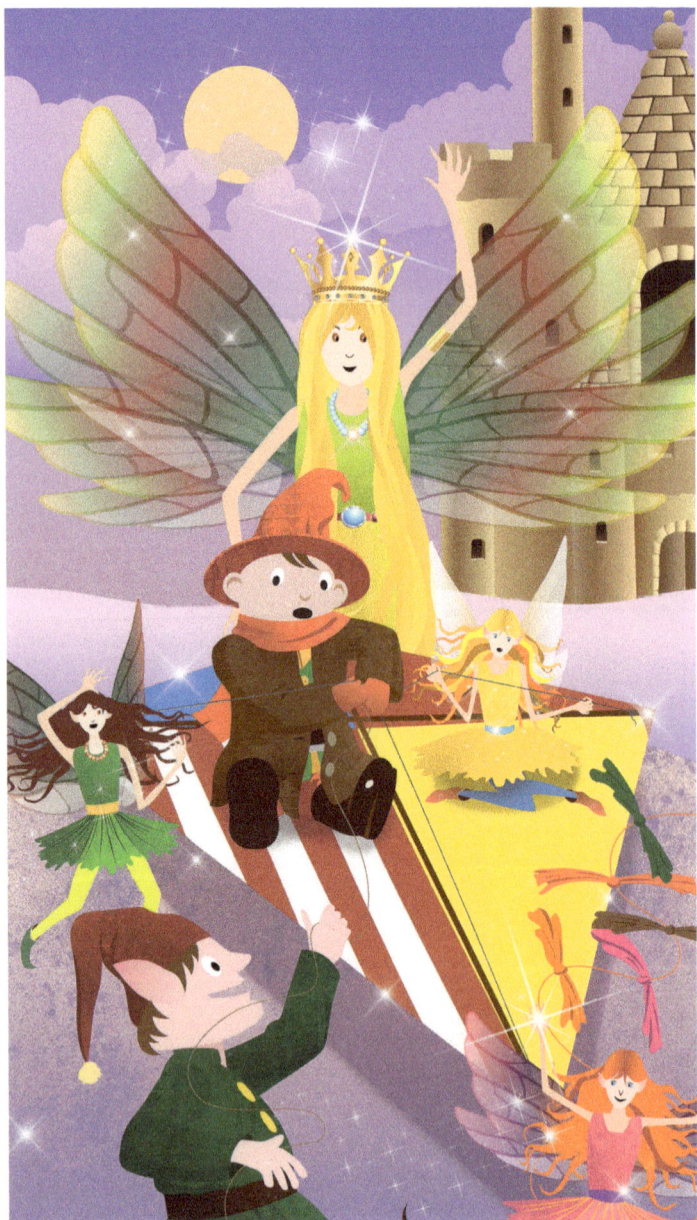

MARCH

Hello, Jerome, are you going to play?
Tell me what's happening – what you'll do today.

◎◎

Jerome he got up and wanted to play.
The sun it shone bright on this windy March day.
He had found in his toy box his favourite kite.
It was yellow and blue with stripes red and white.

He put on his coat, his scarf and his gloves
And walked to the park which he really loves.
The park is the place where his kite he can fly
Up in the big, blue, wide open sky.

Jerome he was busy unpacking his kite
When suddenly he saw a bright shining light.
There on the seat, on this bright sunny day,
Was his best fairy friend; she's called Lucy-May.

'What fun we can have!' she shouted with glee.
'Your kite will fly high – to the top of the tree.
Come hold my hand, let's sit on the kite.'
The wind picked them up; the friends held on tight.

The kite it flew up high into the sky.
Jerome and the fairy were flying so high.
They looked down below and oh! What a sight!
They couldn't believe their magical flight.

Instead of the park, where they had just been,
Was the land of the fairies and the Wood Fairy Queen.
Jerome had been told of this land far away,
But what a surprise to be here today.

The kite floated down to the grass and the flowers,
And there on the hill was a castle with towers.
The Wood Fairy Castle was there on the hill.
'I am sure we can visit, but just sit here quite still.'

The fairy she knew that if they would wait
A wood elf would take them right up to the gate.
Within a few minutes the elf did arrive.
A carriage of flowers was what he did drive.

The friends got on board and the elf with a smile
Said, 'Hello, I will show you around for a while.'
The carriage of flowers floated just off the ground.
It moved like a cloud, not making a sound.

On the way to the castle they passed by a stream.
The trees they were silver with leaves shiny green.
The elf stopped the carriage; the friends they got out.
The gnome and the fairy wandered about,

Looking at flowers of purple and pink.
They scooped from the stream some water to drink.
The water was sweet and tasted so good,
They probably drank much more than they should.

The elf called them over and said, 'We must go.
The Wood Fairy Queen will be waiting, you know.'
They climbed on the carriage and floated along.
The elf, in the front, was singing a song.

The castle gates opened and to their surprise
The Wood Fairy Queen stood in front of their eyes.
Her long golden hair reached down to the ground.
All the fairy folk watched, not making a sound.

Jerome and the fairy were brought to the Queen.
What a wonderful sight, in her dress golden green.
What a magical sight; how lucky they'd been
To visit the castle and the Wood Fairy Queen.

The fairy folk sang and danced through the day
And soon it was time to be on their way.
The Queen called them over to stand on a square.
Jerome and the fairy were quite unaware

The square that they stood on was really the kite.
The Queen waved her wand and it lifted in flight.
It hovered above the ground for a while,
And all the wood fairies waved with a smile.

'Off you must go, back home,' said the Queen.
'This magical journey will be but a dream.'
The kite it flew off, back up in the sky.
The two little friends they waved their goodbye.

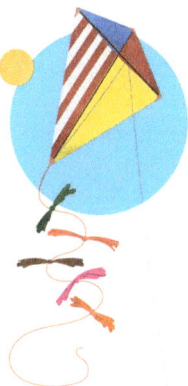

Before very long they saw the old tree.
The kite floated down and the park they could see.
Jerome and the fairy packed up the kite.
What a magical day and a wonderful sight:

The Wood Fairy Queen in her magical land.
A day like today they could never have planned.
Now it was time for Jerome to go home
To dream of the place that they had just flown.

�☉☉

Goodbye, Jerome, thanks for sharing your day,
For letting me know the things that you play.

Thank you for
helping me x

APRIL

Hello, Jerome, are you going to play?
Tell me what's happening – what you'll do today.

◎◎

Today the sun's shining, there are no April showers.
The birds and the bees all play in the flowers.
Jerome is excited, for it's special, you see.
There's chocolate been left by the Easter Bunny.

Chocolate cake and chocolate eggs,
Chocolate bunnies with chocolate legs.
Jerome eats his breakfast and goes out to play.
His nanny and granddad will come later that day.

At Easter, you see, the gnomes all have lunch,
With their favourite food and chocolate to munch.
Jerome he went out to sit in the sun,
To watch baby birds and rabbits have fun.

This is the time the grown-ups call spring
When everything grows and baby birds sing.
The gnome he was sat in the grass by a tree
When all of a sudden – oh! Dear me.

A baby bird landed by his feet with a thud,
His little wings broken and covered in mud.
Jerome he got up to help the poor thing.
'Don't cry, baby bird. Let me look at your wing.

'What's happened to you? You're covered in dirt.'
'I know,' said the bird, 'and my wing it does hurt.'
'Come on, let me take you down to the stream.
We can give you a wash and get you all clean.'

Jerome washed the bird to make him feel better.
The bird asked Jerome for his mum. 'Can you get her?'
'Let me think,' said Jerome, 'what's the best I can do.
I don't want to leave you, a baby so new.'

Jerome made a nest from moss and some sticks.
He needed his friend; her magic would fix
The baby bird's wings, and then he could fly
Back to his mummy way up in the sky.

Jerome he turned round, and there by the tree
Was his best fairy friend. She had just come to see
What Jerome was doing on this fine Easter day.
She hoped he would be there so they could both play.

'I'm so pleased to see you – look what I've found:
A new baby bird, he fell on the ground.
His wings are all broken, come look and see.
He's a sad little bird; can you come and help me?'

The fairy she looked at the poor little thing.
With a swish of her wand she mended the wings.
The little bird hopped around on the ground,
Then fluttered his wings and flew all around.

Jerome and the fairy they danced in the sun
And the little bird flew back home to his mum.
'Thank you so much for helping the bird.
Please come back for tea; as you may have heard,

My nanny and granddad are coming for tea.
I would love you to come and meet them with me.'
The gnome and the fairy made their way back
To find that Jerome had been left a large sack!

The sack it was full of chocolate and things
With love from the bird for mending his wings.
The chocolate was good; they all had too much,
Even the rabbit, sat out in his hutch.

Soon Easter day ended and they all had to go.
What a wonderful day. Now, with the sun low,
The gnomes said farewell and, waving goodbye,
Jerome looked up, and there in the sky

Was a small flock of birds all singing in tune.
Jerome looked and waved and called, 'See you soon,
For now I am tired, it's been such a long day,
But tomorrow I'll come to the forest and play.'

☺☺

Goodbye, Jerome, thanks for sharing your day,
For letting me know the things that you play.

23

MAY

◎◎

Jerome woke excited as today he would be
Meeting his fairy friends out for his tea.
Before he could go he had jobs to do,
Help weed the garden and paint the shed blue.

There is plenty to do for the garden to grow,
Like plant lots of seeds, all in a row.
May is the time when Jerome has such fun
Watching his fairy friends dance in the sun.

They set up a pole high in the sky and tie
Coloured ribbons on the top, very high.
Taking a ribbon, they each hold on tight.
They dance in and out; some even take flight.

The ribbons are woven around and around,
The fairy folk dance and the pole is all bound
With a rainbow of colours from bottom to top.
The fairies all sing and dance till they drop.

The fairy folk, tired and ready to eat,
Have a picnic with goodies – oh! What a treat.
Jerome joined his friends; they sat by the stream.
There were cookies and muffins and even ice cream.

Lucy-May and Jerome they ate until full.
They had party hats, poppers and crackers to pull.
The two friends they went and paddled their feet.
They walked by the stream and sat on the seat.

They watched all the fairies dance round the Maypole
When to their surprise came along Mr Mole.
'Hello,' said the fairy. 'Are you feeling OK?
It's not normal to see you at this time of day.'

'Well, to tell you the truth, things are not good.
I got up too early, then got lost in the wood.
I eventually found my way to the stream,
Then followed it here – it's hours I've been.

'I've been walking and walking to find my way back
To the lane that leads to the old farmyard track.
The problem I have is that I cannot see.
I've mislaid my glasses and oh! Dear me.

'I've searched and I've searched, which is why I got lost.
I even dug round the garden compost.
So you see, little friends, I need to go home,
But I'm not sure I'll get there if I go on my own.'

The two little friends, they stood one each side,
Took Mr Mole's hands and said, 'Come, we will ride.'
There by the stream stood a pony of white,
Pulling a carriage with a seat in – just right.

The friends and the mole climbed upon board,
And there by the pony was an elf with a sword.
'I am a knight of the Wood Fairy Queen
And have been sent to help, as the Queen she has seen
With her magical powers that you need a ride,
So please all sit down now that you are inside'.

The mole and Jerome and Lucy-May too
All sat in the carriage without further to do.
The knight elf on board raised his sword in the air;
With a few magic words the carriage was there.

In front of them stood Mr Mole's house
And waiting outside was a little black mouse.
'Hello, Mr Mole, I am pleased that you're back,
For while I was out down the old farmyard track,
I suddenly came upon these by the tree.
I looked and I thought, "Now what could these be?"'

'Why, it's Mr Mole's glasses,' said Jerome and the elf.
The mouse brought them over so he could see for himself.
'Oh, thanks, little mouse; I've been unable to see.
How kind of you to return them to me.'

'No trouble at all,' said the little black mouse.
'I was so pleased to find you here at your house.
I really must go now, I have to get tea.
Mrs Mouse and the children will be waiting for me.'

Lucy-May and Jerome said goodbye to the mole;
He put on his glasses and went back down his hole.
The pony and carriage were ready to go.
'Come on,' said the elf. 'I have something to show.'

Jerome and the fairy were soon on their way.
Where was the elf going on this sunny May Day?
They went down the farm track, then down by the stream,
Then into the forest with trees tall and green.
There in the forest was a wonderful sight,
The Wood Fairy Queen with her wings shining bright.

The Fairy Queen sang a beautiful song.
The fairy folk listened and before very long
With the wave of her wand the Queen cast a spell;
A shower of stars and diamonds fell.

The stars and the diamonds each hit the ground,
And where every one landed a fairy was found.
Lucy-May told Jerome that this was the way
That new little fairies were born on May Day.

'Come,' said the elf, 'it's now time to go,
For it's getting late and the way home I must show.'
The little friends thanked the elf for the treat,
For letting them see the new fairies so sweet.

They waved their goodbyes and headed on home;
Another adventure for little Jerome.

◎◎

Goodbye, Jerome, thanks for sharing your day,
For letting me know the things that you play.

JUNE

Hello, Jerome, are you going to play?
Tell me what's happening – what you'll do today.

◎◎

The grass is so long and the flowers in bloom,
The sun shines so bright on a June afternoon.
This is the time when Jerome wants to play
With his best fairy friend – she's called Lucy-May.

Jerome asks his mum, 'Can I go out to play?
Can I go on my bike and find Lucy-May?'
'Of course you can go, but just you make sure
That you take a packed lunch and you're back here at four.'

Lucy-May she was waiting by the pond in the sun.
She was all ready to play with Jerome and have fun.
They laughed and they played and climbed the big tree,
But soon it was time to go home for their tea.

'I have had so much fun,' declared Lucy-May.
'I really do wish we had more time to play.'
But they both knew the rules and so they must hurry
Back to their homes so their mums wouldn't worry.

The friends said farewell with a hug and a kiss.
They promised to meet and have more days like this.
Lucy-May waved her wand – with a whoosh, she was home.
Jerome, on his bike, pedalled home all alone.

Jerome's mummy waiting by the gate, she could see
A tired little gnome coming home for his tea.
'I've had so much fun with my friend Lucy-May.
She's my very best friend – can she come over and stay?'

'We will speak to her mummy in the morning and see,
But now you get washed and ready for tea.'
Jerome had his tea and got ready for bed.
He put on his PJs; they were blue, white and red.

Jerome was so tired; he'd had such a fun day,
And tomorrow his best friend was coming to stay.

Early next morning Lucy-May came to play.
It was just after breakfast on a bright sunny day.
Lucy-May she arrived with her bag in her hand.
Jerome couldn't wait to tell what he'd planned.

First they would have a picnic for lunch,
Strawberry crumble and apples to munch.
The picnic lunch eaten, it was now time to go.
They walked hand in hand to a place they both know.

The friends soon arrived at Buttercup Glade,
Where fairy folk meet, by the pond in the shade,
A butterfly waiting to give them a ride,
Lucy-May so excited with Jerome by her side.

The butterfly took them up high, then down low.
They saw all the places only fairy folk know.
The friends they were taken back to Jerome's home.
They thanked Butterfly for the places he'd flown.

Soon the two friends were tucked up for the night
To chat and remember their magical flight.

◎◎

Goodbye, Jerome, thanks for sharing your day,
For letting me know the things that you play.

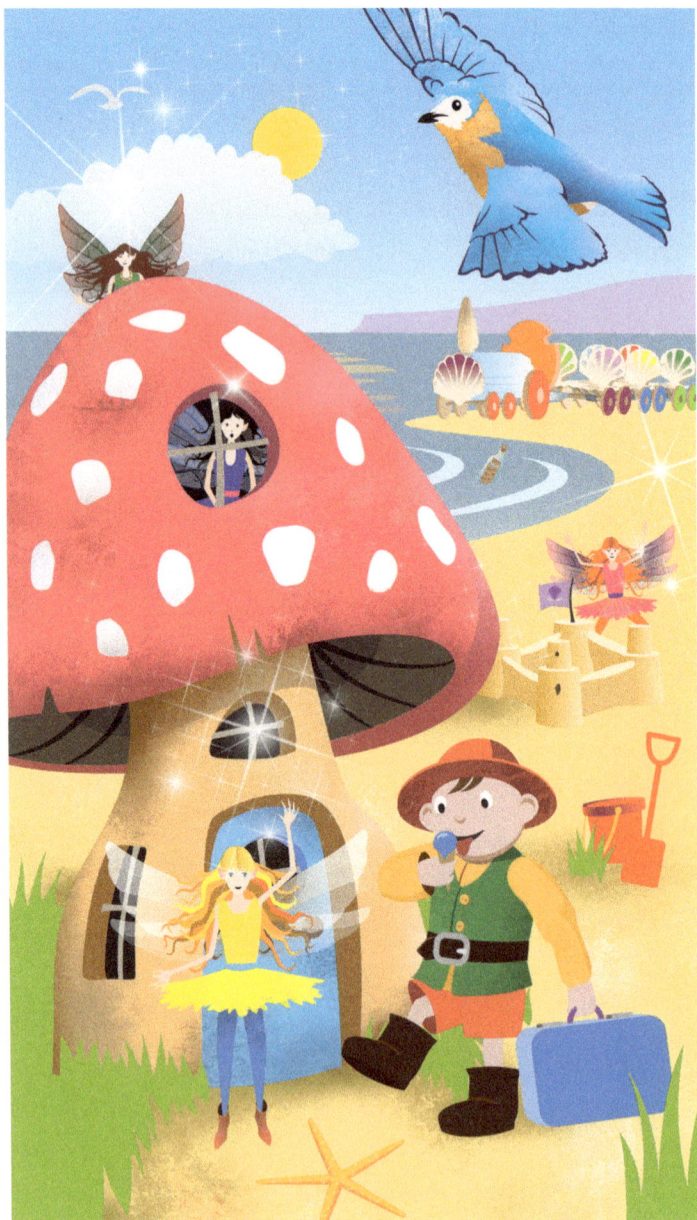

JULY

Hello, Jerome, are you going to play?
Tell me what's happening – what you'll do today.

◎◎

Today Jerome's busy; he's packing his case.
He's going on holiday to a far-away place.
He's put in his shorts, his sun hat and cream.
Today he is going where he's never been.

He's heard of the beach that goes down to the sea
And later that day it's where he will be.
Jerome and his friend Lucy-May will both fly
On the back of a bluebird way up in the sky.

The bluebird will take them to a house on the sand
Where fairy folk stay for their holidays planned.
The bluebird is ready; on her back is a seat.
The friends settle down and her wings gently beat.

The bird she takes flight way up in the sky.
Jerome and the fairy look down from up high.
They fly over the forest and follow the stream,
Then start seeing places that they've never seen.

The stream it gets wider the further they go.
They see lots of seagulls and the fairy friends know
That soon they will be by the beach and the sea.
The bluebird she lands in the grass by a tree.

The two little friends thank the bird for the ride;
How excited they are to be at the seaside.
They unpack their bags and get ready to go
On a train made of seashells, and the fairies all know
That the train takes them down to the wide open sea
Where they can play on the beach and have ice-cream tea.

Jerome he has fun making things in the sand;
They play in the sea and do all that they planned.
It is on their last day when a bottle they find,
With a message inside saying, 'I hope that you're kind.

'I am a gnome and I'm stuck in the sand.
I really do need some help and a hand.
I was climbing the rocks when I suddenly fell,
And now I am cold and not feeling too well.'

Jerome and the fairy started searching around
And before very long the gnome he was found.
The gnome was so pleased to see the two friends.
'I hoped the bottle and the message it sends
Would not float away in the wide open sea,
But send someone kind to come and help me.'

Before very long the gnome, safe and sound,
Was having some ice cream and running around.
The rest of the day they played with their friend
For tomorrow was time for the holiday to end.

They made a sandcastle; it reached to the sky.
They played and they laughed and ate blueberry pie.
What fun the three had on the beach by the sea,
The sun shining bright, just like summer should be.

Soon it was time for the friends to go back.
They said their goodbyes, for they had to pack.
Jerome and the fairy slept soundly that night,
Their cases all packed for the next morning flight.

The bluebird arrived in the grass by the tree.
Lucy-May and Jerome, the bluebird could see,
Were saying goodbye from the train made of shells;
There were fairies and gnomes all shouting farewells.

The friends settled down in their seat for the flight.
The bluebird she flew them, the sun shining bright,
Over the beach and down to the sea
To the place where the castle they'd made would still be.

The castle was standing so tall and so proud
And stood all around were their friends shouting loud,
'Goodbye, little friends, please come back real soon.'
They waved as the bluebird she sang a sweet tune.

Lucy-May and Jerome settled down for the flight
And they flew through the sky with clouds fluffy white.
'I do love the beach with the sea and the sand,'
Said Jerome as he held on to Lucy-May's hand.

'Me too,' said the fairy. 'We must come back one day
To meet our new friends – oh, I wish we could stay.'

The friends they both knew that they must go home
To share their adventure of the beach and the gnome
Who sent out a message of help to the friends
And how they both helped and it happily ends.

@@

Goodbye, Jerome, thanks for sharing your day,
For letting me know the things that you play.

AUGUST

Hello, Jerome, are you going to play?
Tell me what's happening – what you'll do today.

◎◎

Lucy-May was up and ready to play.
She called for Jerome on a sunshiny day.
The friends, they had planned to go down to the park.
They promised to be home before it got dark.

A picnic was packed – to have lunch by the lake.
Jerome's mum had made a big chocolate cake.
They walked down the lane and soon they were near,
When the friends they both stopped as a noise they could
    hear.

'It sounds like music being played over there.'
'Oh, look in the park,' said Jerome. 'It's the fair.'
They ran down the lane as fast as they could.
They took a shortcut and came out by the wood.

They stopped for a rest and had lemonade,
Watched the rides in the fairground, while they sat in the
    shade.
'Oh no,' said the fairy, 'we can't go to the fair.
We need to have money for the rides over there.'

'Let me think,' said Jerome. 'There must be a way
That we can have fun at the fair here today.'
The friends looked around until they came to the lake.
They found a small boat and a ride they did take.

Jerome rowed the boat until his arms ached.
'Let's have some cake that my mummy has baked.'
'That's a good plan,' Lucy-May said with glee.
'You can rest your tired arms; come sit here with me.'

Jerome he stood up to sit with his friend.
The boat rocked and swayed as he walked to the end.
The boat it then tipped and the chocolate cake fell
Straight into the lake, and the oars went as well.

'Oh no!' Jerome cried. 'What shall we do now?
There's no oars to paddle and I don't know how
We can get back to land without getting wet.'
'Don't worry, Jerome, there's no need to fret.'

Lucy-May she had her magical powers
And before very long the lake turned to flowers.
The two little friends jumped out of the boat
As it was no longer on water and it didn't float.

'It's amazing,' Jerome said as he looked around
When there in the flowers the cake it was found.
'Oh, it would be fun if we could just ride
On one of those merry-go-rounds – side by side.

'How can we do that with no money to pay?'
'I'll do fairy magic, then we can both play
On a wonderful roundabout I will now make
Out of our very own chocolate cake.'

Jerome stood and watched and to his surprise
The cake it grew big in front of his eyes.
The chocolate all melted away and there stood
A musical roundabout – all made of wood.

The two friends they climbed on board for a ride.
They each had a pony which they sat astride.
'Hold tight,' said the fairy, 'for I think you will see
That the ponies are magic and will take you and me

'For a magical ride round the lake made of flowers.'
The friends they had fun for hours and hours.
The ponies they took the friends high and low.
They went to the places they wanted to go.

At the end of the day, the sun soon to set,
The ponies they knew that they had to get
Back to the cake that was now made of wood.
They flew though the sky as fast as they could.

The friends led the ponies back to the cake.
With a swish of her wand the fairy did make
The roundabout turn to chocolate again
And before very long they were back down the lane.

They walked past the field where they'd seen the fair
That had been playing music, but was no longer there.
Lucy-May said farewell to her best friend Jerome.
She blew him a kiss and then flew off home.

Jerome walked on home just in time for his tea.
His mum had been baking – oh, what could it be?
There on the plate was a round chocolate cake
With ponies of chocolate his mum she did make.

The little gnome looked at the cake with a smile.
He sat and he thought of the fair for a while.
Would his mum laugh if he told of his day,
How he and his friend on the ponies did play?

He decided to eat his tea and not say
Of his magical day with his friend Lucy-May.

◎◎

Goodbye, Jerome, thanks for sharing your day,
For letting me know the things that you play.

SEPTEMBER

Hello, Jerome, are you going to play?
Tell me what's happening – what you'll do today.

◎◎

The summer was soon to come to an end.
Lucy-May and Jerome had made a new friend.
The fairy and gnome met their friend out one day
When they went to the park where they always play.

Gerald the elf had come from afar.
He now lived down the lane with his ma and his pa.
Today the three friends were all clean and neat.
They were ready for school; by the wood they would meet.

They met at the wood to walk down the lane,
Their uniforms white and green all the same.
The friends walked on quickly; they mustn't be late.
The teacher would be there stood by the school gate.

Jerome he loved school; he learnt lots of things.
Lucy-May was taught how to look after her wings.
Gerald the elf was shown how to be good
At making new toys out of old bits of wood.

The friends they met up each day after school.
Sometimes they went for a swim in the pool.
At the weekends the friends would all hope to meet
In the park down the lane on their favourite seat.

Saturdays were the days they had the most fun
Laughing and playing around in the sun.
This was the time when the whole school would go
To the very big tree where the conkers would grow.

The fairies and pixies, the elves and the gnomes
All went to find conkers to take back to their homes.
Everyone threaded their conkers on strings.
The hardest stays whole when it hits and it swings.

Today was the day when the three friends they met
In the playground, all ready the conkers to get.
The teacher she got them all lined up in twos.
They walked in a line, their conkers to choose.

It had not been too long when they all reached the tree
And everyone gasped, 'Oh no – dear me.'
Not one single conker could be seen on the ground.
Everyone looked up, not making a sound.

The tree it stood tall, its branches all bare.
Not one single conker did the tree have to share.
Each elf, gnome and pixie looked on in dismay.
What would they do now with no conkers to play?
Lucy-May she took flight to the top of the tree
To try and find out what the problem could be.
The fairy landed on the branches so high.
The tree came to life and with a big sigh
Told the fairy how all her conkers had gone.
Each one of them fell to the ground one by one.

'You see,' said the tree, 'the Wood Witch has been.
I heard of her plan to harm the Wood Queen.
She needed the conkers to use in her spell,
So when she moved on I knew very well
That all I could do to stop the old Witch
Was to get all the conkers to hide in the ditch.

'The Witch will return very soon, I am sure,
In hope of collecting the conkers she saw.
I think she'll be cross when she comes back to see
No conkers remain; there's just a bare tree.'

The Witch she returned to the tree where she'd been
To get all the conkers that she had once seen.
To her surprise no conkers were there.
She looked at the tree with a sinister glare.

'What have you done with the conkers you had?
I need them to use in my spell – now I'm mad.
The potion will turn the Wood Queen into stone,
Then the wood will be mine, for me on my own.

'There will be no more laughing and fun in the wood.
I will cast a big spell, make a river of mud
To stop all the fairies, pixies and elves
Coming to the wood and enjoying themselves.'

Lucy-May she could hear what the old Witch had planned.
She thought quickly and with the wave of her hand
The conkers all flew from out of the ditch
And started to chase the old wicked Witch.
The wicked Witch ran as fast as she could.
She ran and she ran out of the wood.

The Wood Fairy Queen came to thank Lucy-May
For saving the wood from the old Witch that day.
The big conker tree still stands in the wood
And each year she grows large conkers so good.

The fairies and pixies and the elves too
Try to find the best conkers, just like we all do.
The fairy folk friends chose their conkers that day.
They laughed and they played and thanked Lucy-May.

Gerald the elf made a dish out of wood
And Jerome had made cookies, the best that he could.
The big dish of cookies was shared by the friends,
Then they all went back home as another day ends.

◎◎

Goodbye, Jerome, thanks for sharing your day,
For letting me know the things that you play.

OCTOBER

Hello, Jerome, are you going to play?
Tell me what's happening – what you'll do today.

֎֎

Gerald the elf and Lucy-May too
Were going to meet Jerome at the zoo.
The friends had arranged to go for the day
To watch all their favourite animals play.

Gerald he liked the chimps and the apes.
They all stood and watched and fed them some grapes.
Lucy-May's favourite place was the butterfly house.
The three friends they sat all as quiet as a mouse.

Jerome he just loved to see the rhinos.
They trundle around with a horn on their nose.
The three friends they saw all manner of things,
The lions and tigers and a big bird that sings.

They saw lizards and snakes and crocodiles too,
Sea lions, penguins and frogs of bright blue.
Jerome and his friends had a wonderful day
And while taking a rest planned some tricks they could play

For when they got home and just after tea
They were all to dress up and scary must be.
The friends had grown pumpkins, the best they had seen.
They carved them with faces for today – Halloween.

Lucy-May and Jerome liked to do trick-or-treats.
They went round the neighbours and got lots of sweets.
Gerald the elf dressed up like a ghost.
He frightened his friends – Lucy-May was scared most.

They had so much fun on that October night.
They even gave the Wood Witch a bit of a fright.
The friends all had fun in the light of the moon.
The bats and the owls would all be out soon.

Jerome and his friends were all getting sleepy.
The sky was now dark and everything creepy.
Lucy-May she was tired, said goodnight to Jerome.
With the wave of her wand she was on her way home.

Gerald the elf, dressed like a ghost in a sheet,
Said goodnight to Jerome and his mother did meet.
Jerome made his way back home in the dark,
Said goodnight to the owl as he walked past the park.

Jerome was soon home to tell of his day,
The trip to the zoo with his friend Lucy-May,
The Halloween tricks and Gerald the ghost.
He didn't know which part he had liked the most.

⊚⊚

Goodbye, Jerome, thanks for sharing your day,
For letting me know the things that you play.

NOVEMBER

Hello, Jerome, are you going to play?
Tell me what's happening – what you'll do today.

◎◎

Jerome he was busy down in the shed.
He was making a Guy – a mop for his head.
The friends had been gathering old bits of wood.
A bonfire tall in the garden now stood.

Lucy-May and Jerome they loved Bonfire Night
With fireworks, sparklers and rockets so bright.
The 5th of November was soon to be here
When all of their friends came to watch and to cheer.

Jerome's mum and dad had a firework display,
Then a firework party, at which they would stay.

There were hot dogs and burgers and steaming hot soup.
Everyone stood, to keep warm, in a group.
With woolly hats on and coats done up tight
They would watch as the fireworks lit up the night.

After the last rocket had lit up the sky
The bonfire was lit and on top was the Guy.
Everyone cheered as the fire caught alight.
It made a red glow in the dark of the night.

Sparklers were given to everyone there.
Marshmallows on sticks were toasted to share.
The warmth from the fire made faces go red.
The little ones, tired, went home to their bed.

The old friends danced holding hands in a ring.
The mums and the dads all started to sing,
Then suddenly up in the sky very dark
Was a very bright light that lit up the park.

The Wood Fairy Queen appeared on the ground,
Then told of her journey and what she had found.
Way up high in the sky, past the stars and the moon,
She came to a place where the clouds played a tune.

Every cloud in the sky was misty and grey.
Each one was a home for a Guy Fawkes to stay,
For this was the land where all Guy Fawkes go.
When the bonfires are lit and the smoke it does blow
Way up in the sky to make clouds misty grey,
The Guys they all meet and they dance and they play.

With the wave of her hand a grey mist it came down,
Then it lifted again and there, all stood in brown,
Were all of the Guy Fawkes that everyone made.
They sang and they danced, they laughed and they played.

Well into the night the party went on,
Then the Wood Fairy Queen she spotted the sun.
'I'm afraid it is time for the Guys to go back
To their home in the sky – I will make a smoke track

'So you can all find your way to your cloud in the sky.'
The Guys turned to smoke as they all waved goodbye.
Lucy-May and Jerome were happy to know
That each Guy they made had somewhere to go.

The Wood Fairy Queen she went with the Guys.
The bright light went out in front of their eyes.
The elves and the gnomes were left in the dark.
They all headed home back through the park.

Another magical night for little Jerome.
He remembered the Guy that he'd made at home.
He had seen his own Guy with a mop for a head.
He had been singing and dancing and to Jerome said,

'Thanks for making me for your Bonfire Night,
For letting me sit and burn up so bright.
I turned into smoke and went high in the sky
And live in the clouds past the stars very high.'

Jerome was soon home and tucked up in bed.
He thought of his Guy and the things he had said.
What fun to live up on a cloud past the moon
Where the Wood Fairy Queen said the clouds played a tune.

'Perhaps when I'm older I may get to see
All the Guy Fawkes I've made, who live so happy
Up in the sky on clouds misty grey.
Maybe I'll go with my friend Lucy-May.'

@@

Goodbye, Jerome, thanks for sharing your day,
For letting me know the things that you play.

DECEMBER

Hello, Jerome, are you going to play?
Tell me what's happening – what you'll do today.

๏๏

Lucy-May and Jerome were down in the wood
Finding a Christmas tree; it had to be good.
It was the time when the gnomes, fairies and elves
Were all very good and behaving themselves,

For in a few weeks it would be Christmas Day
And soon all the elves would be taken away.
The Wood Fairy Queen appeared in the night.
She took all the elves on a magical flight.

They went to a place that only she knew
Where the elves would make presents for me and for you.
In this land far away lives our friend Santa Claus.
It was there that our elves helped with all of the chores.

Some would make teddy bears, some would make trains.
There were dolls' houses, bicycles, jigsaws and planes.
The elves were kept busy from morning till night
Preparing for Santa to make his Christmas Eve flight.

Lucy-May and Jerome found a Christmas tree tall,
Just right for the fairy and gnome Christmas ball.
Everyone went to this Christmas event.
It was on Christmas Eve in a very big tent.

The tent it was made of cobwebby lace
With sparkling diamonds all over the place.
The fairies and all prepared for the ball.
They took lots of goodies, dressed the Christmas tree tall.

On the day of the party they all dressed up smart,
Arrived at the tent all ready to start.
There was music and dancing and plenty to eat.
Everyone joined in this Christmas Eve treat.

In the cobwebby tent the Christmas tree stood.
The Fairy Queen came as she always would
To light up the tree with her magical powers.
The tree it was covered in glittering flowers.

This was the time when everyone knew
That before very long Santa Claus would be due,
But before he arrived the elves would come back
For they had finished their work and filled Santa's sack.

The Wood Fairy Queen with her magical spell
Made a bright-coloured rainbow from which the elves fell.
They landed quite safely in front of the Queen,
All dressed in coats of silver and green.

The coats, which were magic, the elves had each year
For helping out Santa to spread Christmas cheer.
Before very long the tree lit up bright.
It shone in the dark on this Christmas Eve night.

Everyone waited; they knew it was time
For Santa to come, just as the clocks chime.
There in the dark sky was a star shining bright.
The fairy folk knew what it meant on that night.

It was a star that lit up a new fairy's home.
She lived on a moonbeam; it was there she was flown.
The fairy was special; she had magical wings,
A fairy princess that dances and sings.

The Fairy Queen cast her magical spell
And from the bright star a new fairy fell.
The Fairy Princess had long golden hair.
Her wings' rainbow colours made everyone stare.

Jerome and his friend both stood quite amazed
While the Fairy Princess her wand she did raise,
Changed her wings to feathers, then doves that took flight.
The two birds flew off into the dark night.

Before very long the doves they came back,
Bringing back with them a snowy white sack.
The sack it was placed by the tall Christmas tree.
The fairy folk watched, for they knew it would be

The magical sack filled with fairy folk toys,
Just like Santa's red sack for all good girls and boys.
The white sack it grew as big as the tree,
Then it burst open wide and the presents set free.

They flew through the air way up in the sky,
Then started to float down from the clouds way up high.
Each fairy and gnome and all of the elves,
Each had a present all to themselves.

The presents once landed, the white sack was gone
And there stood Santa with his jolly face on.
'Merry Christmas,' he shouted, 'and now I must go
To deliver more presents out there in the snow.'

Santa flew off with his reindeer and sleigh.
He waved to the fairies as he flew away.
The Fairy Princess had her wings once again.
They shone like two rainbows in a warm summer rain.

Everyone watched as a bright star appeared.
It scooped up the princess and everyone cheered.
The Fairy Princess had to be on her way
Back to the moonbeam before Christmas Day.

Lucy-May and Jerome each had their new gift.
They stood by a toadstool to wait for a lift.
Along came a glow-worm to give them a ride.
They climbed in the carriage and sat side by side.

'Where to?' said the glow-worm. 'Are you going home?'
'Yes, please,' they called back. 'To my house,' said Jerome.
They arrived at the gate; Lucy-May blew a kiss.
'What fun I have had on this eve of Christmas.'

The two friends both knew that they had to go
Home to their beds, as Santa would know
That he could not visit with his reindeer and sleigh
Until everyone slept before Christmas Day.

Soon there was silence all through the wood.
Santa he came to all those who were good.
He left presents for all the fairies and gnomes,
All the children and parents asleep in their homes.

When his big sack was empty he knew he was done.
He had delivered his presents, it had been so much fun,
But now it was time for Santa to go.
His reindeer and sleigh took him out in the snow.

The snow it fell thick, left a blanket of white.
'Merry Christmas!' he called, flying into the night.
Early next morning the fairy folk found
That the snow had appeared and covered the ground.

Santa had been with gifts for them all.
Some presents were big, some very small.
Lucy-May and Jerome and all their friends too
Send big Christmas wishes especially to you.

◎◎

Goodbye Jerome, thanks for sharing your day,
For letting me know the things that you play.

Lightning Source UK Ltd.
Milton Keynes UK
UKHW051118281018
331341UK00004B/13/P

9 781911 589761